THIS WALKER BOOK BELONGS TO:

_____

_____

Very, Well
Done!

For Barbara, who makes bears
S.H.

For Edward (Teddy) Craig
H.C.

First published 1986 by Walker Books Ltd
87 Vauxhall Walk, London SE11 5HJ

This edition published 2003

4 6 8 10 9 7 5

Text © 1986 Sarah Hayes
Illustrations © 1986 Helen Craig Ltd

The right of Sarah Hayes and Helen Craig to be identified as author
and illustrator respectively of this work has been asserted by them
in accordance with the Copyright, Designs and Patents Act 1988

This book has been typeset in Garamond

Printed in China

British Library Cataloguing in Publication Data: a catalogue record
for this book is available from the British Library.

ISBN-13: 978-0-7445-9481-2
ISBN-10: 0-7445-9481-2

wwww.walkerbooks.co.uk

This is the
BEAR

Sarah Hayes illustrated by **Helen Craig**

WALKER BOOKS
AND SUBSIDIARIES
LONDON • BOSTON • SYDNEY • AUCKLAND

This is the bear

who fell in the bin.

This is the dog
who pushed him in.

This is the man
who picked up the sack.

This is the driver

who would not come back.

This is the bear
who went to the dump

and fell on the pile
with a bit of a bump.

This is the boy

who took the bus

and went to the dump

to make a fuss.

This is the man
in an awful grump
who searched

and searched
and searched the dump.

This is the bear
all cold and cross

who did not think
he was really lost.

This is the dog
who smelled the smell

of a bone

and a tin

and a bear as well.

This is the man
who drove them home –

the boy, the bear
and the dog with a bone.

This is the bear
all lovely and clean

who did not say
just where he had been.

This is the boy
who knew quite well,

but promised his friend

he would not tell.

And this is the boy
who woke up in the night
and asked the bear
if he felt all right –
and was very surprised
when the bear shouted out,
'How soon can we have
another day out?'

WALKER BOOKS is the world's leading
independent publisher of children's books.
Working with the best authors and illustrators
we create books for all ages, from babies
to teenagers – books your child will
grow up with and always remember. So…

FOR THE BEST CHILDREN'S BOOKS,
LOOK FOR THE BEAR